Ladies and gentlemen! Boys and girls!
Here, for the first time, I present my new song,

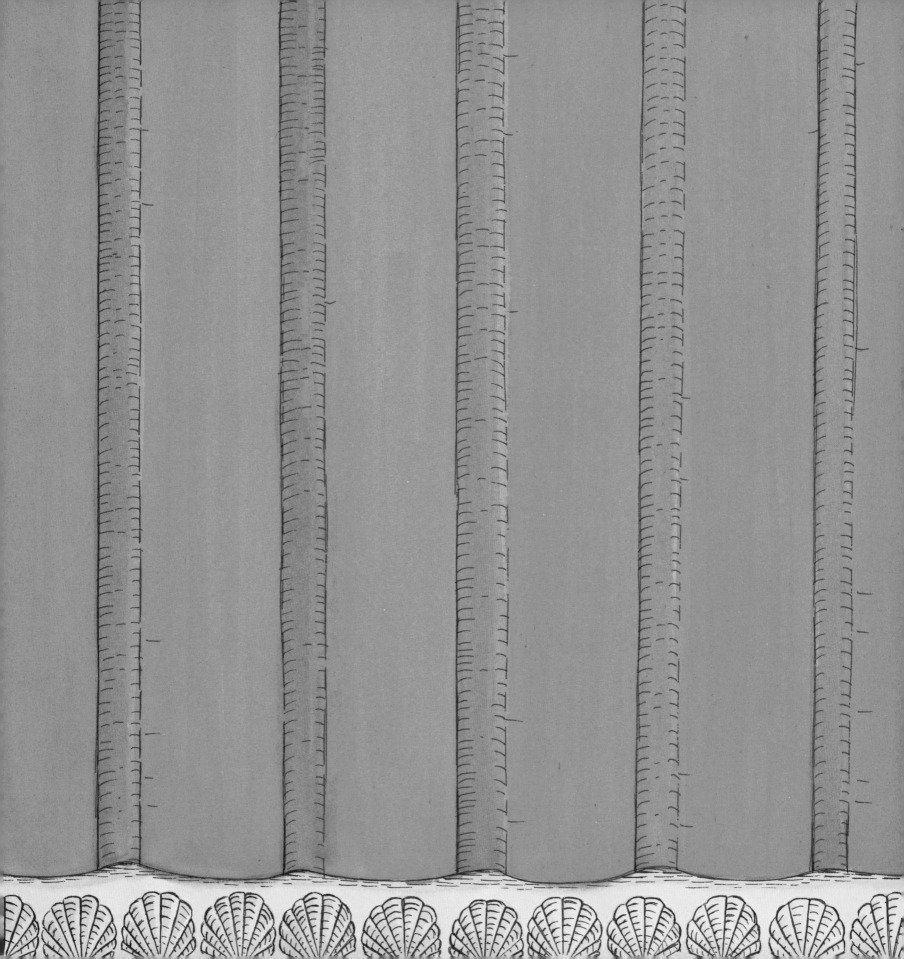

"What Animals Like Most."
A-one, a-two, a-one, two, three, and . . .

We are pigeons,
and we like to coo.

We are cows,
and we like to . . .

. . . dig.

We are worms,
and we like to wiggle.

We are warthogs,
and we like to . . .

. . . *blow enormous bubbles.*

We are frogs,
and we like to swim.

We are shrimp,
and we like to ski.

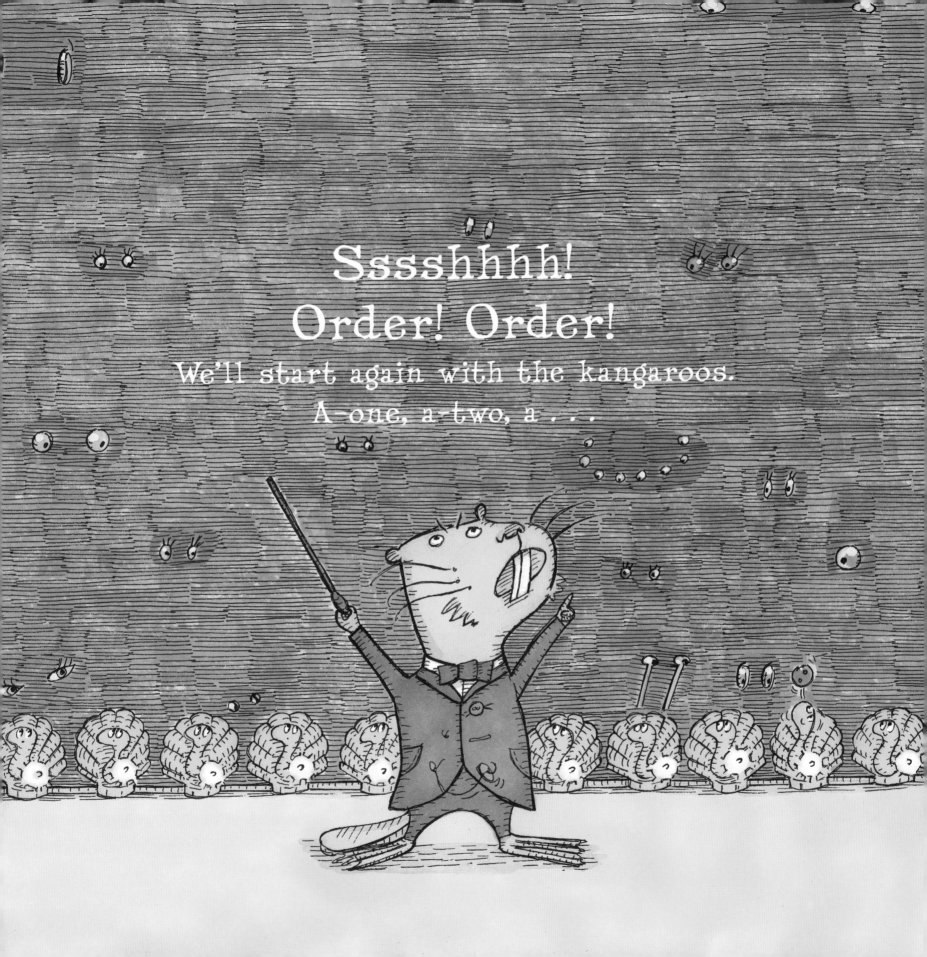

Hmmm. Well, what do *you* think, ladies and gentlemen, boys and girls?
It will probably sound very silly.
And it won't rhyme, you know.
Are you sure you want to hear what the animals really like?
Oh! OK then. From the top. A-one, a-two, a-one, two, three, and . . .

We are lions, and we like . . . flower arranging.

We are cows,
and we like to dig.

We are monkeys,
and we like all-you-can-eat buffets.

We are frogs, and we like tennis and most martial arts. Our favorite food is pizza with extra mushrooms, but with absolutely no tomatoes whatsoever.

We are shrimp, and we like to ski.

Or cheerleading?

Or Modern Art?

No, we really do like cheese!

But most of all we like singing for you!

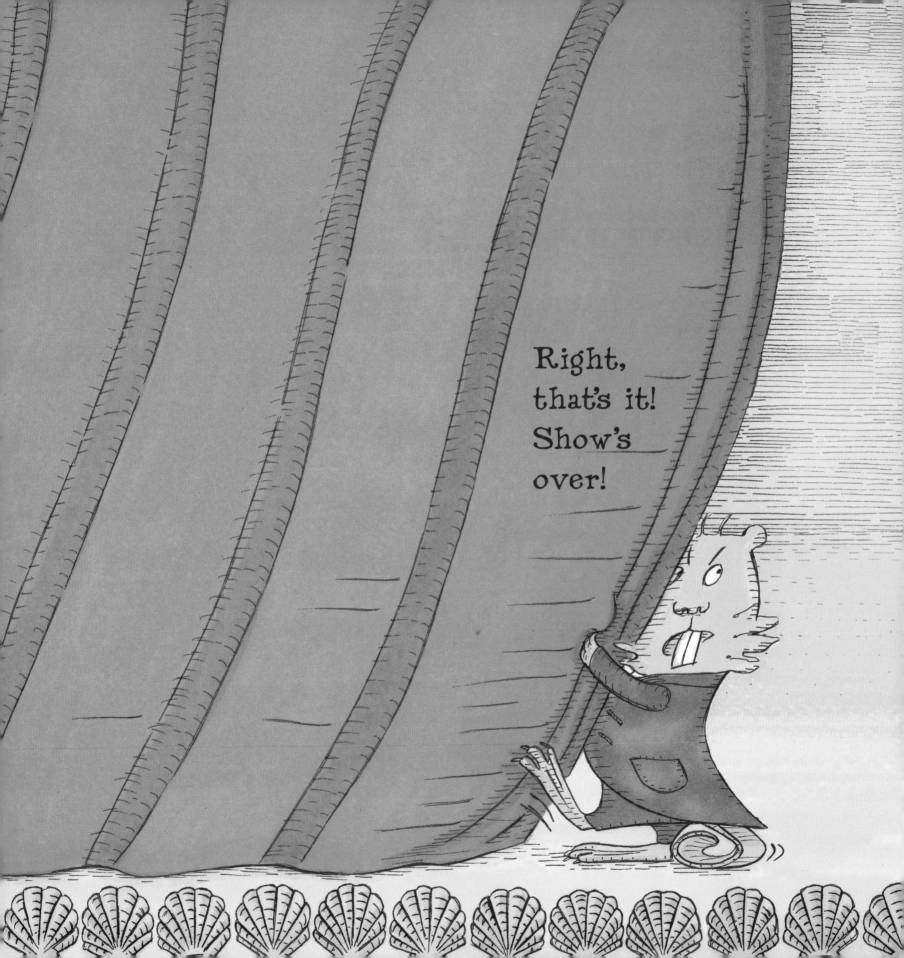

Right,
that's it!
Show's
over!

But I don't like flowers.